HOTEL FLAMINGO

Hotel Flamingo

Hotel Flamingo

Holiday Heat Wave

Carnival Caper

Fabulous Feast

HOTEL FLAMINGO

ALEX MILWAY

First American Edition 2020
Kane Miller, A Division of EDC Publishing

Originally published in the English language as *Hotel Flamingo*
by Piccadilly Press, an imprint of Bonnier Books UK.

For information contact:
Kane Miller, A Division of EDC Publishing
P.O. Box 470663
Tulsa, OK 74147-0663
www.kanemiller.com
www.usbornebooksandmore.com

Library of Congress Control Number: 2019953392

Printed and bound in the United States of America
2 3 4 5 6 7 8 9 10
ISBN: 978-1-68464-126-0

For Arrietty

Port Whisker
Sea Dog
Pirate Tours
Zoozoo Theme Park
Tusks Cinema
Le Chat Shopping Mall
Dukduk Bowling
The Boulevard
Sports Arena
ANIMAL BOULEVARD
Hotel Flamingo
Lookout
Point
Sandy Dunes
Fort Rhino

Whale Holiday Bay
Glowworm Point
Lizard Beach
Artists' Quarter
The Glitz Hotel
Little Fish Marina
Carnival
Opera House
Bush Baby Bay
Bathers' Huts
Welcome to Animal Boulevard
KEY:
Grazing Land
Coastal Path
Watering Hole
HOTEL
FLAMINGO

CAN YOU
FIND ME
IN THE STORY?

Hotel Flamingo

TAXI

1

The Sunniest Hotel in Town

Anna Dupont stepped out of the taxi and saw Hotel Flamingo for the first time.

"Oh, good grief – what a mess!" she said.

Hotel Flamingo was not a pretty sight and was quite unlike the photo in her hand. Its walls were gray and peeling, its windows were cracked, and the revolving door had spun its last.

A large old bear bumped his way through the broken door. He was wearing a bright-red uniform with a tiny red hat, which sat between his large ears.

"Welcome to Hotel Flamingo," said the bear, trying to sound cheerful, "the sunniest hotel in town."

"There's nothing sunny about it," said Anna. "Look at it! Hotel Flamingo is falling apart."

The bear looked sad, as though her words had hurt him.

"What's your name, Mr. Bear?" asked Anna.

"T. Bear, miss," he said gruffly. "I work on the door."

"You mean this place is still open?" said Anna.

"Yes, miss," he replied. "Though we haven't had a guest for three years."

Anna picked up her suitcase and marched toward the door.

"Mr. Bear," she said, "I am the new owner of Hotel Flamingo. Things are going to change around here."

T. Bear stamped to attention. "You're the new boss, miss?" He forced open the broken door with his powerful paw. "After you, miss."

Anna walked into the hotel lobby. The sight made her heart sink. The hotel was as bad inside as out. Cobwebs were draped wall to wall like curtains and a crust of dust covered the carpet. And the smell? Anna couldn't put her finger on it, but she thought the air stank of moldy old socks with a hint of lemon.

She sighed. "We really do have a lot of work to do."

She headed toward the once-grand reception desk, where she found a ring-tailed lemur hunched over the counter. Anna gave his shoulder a very firm poke.

The lemur jumped, his big eyes opening wide.

"Working hard, Mr. Lemmy?" she said, spotting his name badge.

The lemur yawned. "Rushed off my feet," he said, wearily rubbing his eyes.

"So I see," Anna said.

It took a lot of effort to get Lemmy

OFFICE

moving in a morning, but he had an excellent memory for guests and their needs – that was the job of a hotel concierge after all.

"What day is it?" asked Lemmy.

"Excuse me?" said Anna.

It really *had* been a long time since Lemmy had spoken to a guest.

"Sorry," he said, swiping dust from the counter. He opened a large leather-bound guest book and took hold of a pen. "What sort of room would you like, madam? A suite or –"

"A room?" said Anna. "I need an office. This is my hotel! I own it."

"Your hotel?" he asked. He immediately stood more upright and brushed down his uniform.

"That's right," said Anna. "My great-aunt Mathilde left it to me in her will. I'm in charge now."

Lemmy's round eyes opened wider still. "I'm so, so sorry, miss," he said, before pointing to a frosted door behind him. "The office is there, but it's in a bit of a mess . . ."

"This whole place is in a bit of a mess," said Anna. "Where are all the staff? The cleaners? The waiters?"

"They went long ago," said T. Bear, who was pacing around the lobby. "It's just me and Lemmy now, miss. We're all that's left."

Anna shook her head in disapproval. "You

need more than a lemur and a bear to run a hotel," she said.

"We agree, miss," said T. Bear. "But there's no money to pay ourselves, let alone other staff. The safe is empty."

"If you aren't being paid, why are you still here?" she asked.

"Because it's our home," he said warmly. "Always has been, always will be. Hotel Flamingo is in our bones."

If nothing else, Anna could see that T. Bear and Lemmy cared for the hotel. She walked through the lobby, surveying it like the new captain of a ship.

"As of now, it's my home too," said Anna. "And if we all work hard and work together, who knows what we might achieve?"

2

The Grand Tour

The hotel office hadn't been used in years. Portraits of past owners hung on the walls, and Anna even saw a painting of her great-aunt Mathilde frowning down at her. Piles of old paperwork littered the room and stretched from floor to ceiling.

"It's in here somewhere, I know it, miss," grumbled T. Bear, pushing a mountain of envelopes to one side to reveal a desk.

"Thank you," said Anna.

"Here's a chair too," said T. Bear. He lifted up a dirty plant pot to reveal a shabby brown chair.

"What happened to this hotel, Mr. Bear?" asked Anna.

"That's a long, sad story," said T. Bear, who loved to tell a tale. A tear welled in his eye. "We were the only hotel in town until Mr. Ruffian built his mega hotel, the Glitz, up on the hill. They stole all our staff and guests. The Glitz was so shiny, new and exclusive, we couldn't compete."

Anna didn't like the sound of the Glitz, or Mr. Ruffian.

"There must have been something special about this place," said Anna.

"Oh, there was," said T. Bear. "Hotel Flamingo was the friendliest place on Animal Boulevard and, unlike the Glitz, we were open to all creatures – warthogs and all. Even on dark days, the sun would be shining in here."

"The sunniest hotel in town," said Anna.

"That's it, miss," said T. Bear.

"Then that's what we need to bring back," declared Anna. "We need to do what the Glitz can't. We need to be personal, welcoming, and bring the

TiNG!

sunshine back to Animal Boulevard."

Anna got to her feet. "I want the full tour," she said. "Show me everything."

"Everything?" asked T. Bear.

"Nothing less," said Anna.

"Right you are, miss," said T. Bear.

The tour started on the ground floor in the lobby. There was the restaurant, which was filled with old crooked tables but no chairs. Next up was the Piano Lounge, with a carpet so dizzily patterned that it made Anna's head hurt. The piano was missing three keys and was out of tune, but at least there *was* a piano, thought Anna.

From there they ventured outside to the weed-covered garden terrace and its marble-clad swimming pool. The pool was empty and leaked, said T. Bear, though the seabirds enjoyed the puddles in it after a rainstorm.

At the edge of the terrace was a potholed tennis court, its tattered net swinging sadly in the breeze. And past the tennis court was a mound of sand dunes.

"Beyond that lies the sea, miss," said T. Bear. "Because of where the hotel sits on Animal Boulevard, we're lucky to have sea views on both sides of the hotel."

"How perfect," said Anna excitedly. Everyone deserves a sea view from their bedroom, she thought.

The more Anna learned and saw of the hotel, the more she could see the potential.

"And what about the bedrooms?" she asked hopefully.

"There's fifty in total, on five floors, miss," said T. Bear, strolling back inside the hotel. "We have an elevator in the corner of the lobby if you'd like to head that way . . ."

"I think I'd rather take the stairs," said Anna, following him. "The elevator's bound to be broken like everything else in this place . . ."

"Very wise, miss," said T. Bear.

The wide staircase curled up and around to the first floor, splitting in two at its middle.

"The spa is on the third floor," said T. Bear, a little out of breath, "and of course there's the Royal Penthouse up top. But otherwise, the rooms are much the same."

On the first floor T. Bear entered a dark corridor. He switched on the hallway light, and the bulb fizzed before exploding. The hall went dark again, and T. Bear growled sadly in defeat. He found his keys, pawed his way to a door and opened it.

"In you go, miss," he said.

The curtains were open and daylight

poured in. Animal Boulevard stretched out before her. Anna gazed at the brightly colored shops and bustling streets and at the unmistakable splendor of the Glitz up on the hill. Her heart skipped a beat, for there, in the distance, was the sprawling white sandy beach and the glorious shimmering sea.

Animal Boulevard was a rare jewel of a place and so too was Hotel Flamingo, despite its dirty, run-down appearance. With a little bit of work Anna knew it could once again be the best – and sunniest – hotel in town.

Excitement surged through her. "Mr. Bear!" she exclaimed. "All this hotel needs is a little bit of love and care."

"Don't we need to clean it as well, miss?" said T. Bear.

Anna revised her words. "All this hotel needs is a little bit of love, and an awful lot of cleaning," she said. "And we're the people to do it!"

"Yes we are, miss . . ." said T. Bear, a huge smile beaming from his face.

Spring Clean

Anna found a cleaner's cupboard filled with mops, brooms and dusters. She handed them out to Lemmy and T. Bear.

"Mr. Bear, open every door on every floor, and every window you can find," said Anna. "This hotel needs air as much as the rest of us. Blow those cobwebs away. If the spiders aren't paying, get rid of them. And, Lemmy, you and I have some dusting to do. Hotel Flamingo is due a very good spring clean."

"You don't need me on the front desk?" he asked.

Anna wondered if Lemmy was a bit too comfortable at his post.

"Not today," she said. "We've got to get the hotel tidy. Maybe then we'll get our guests back."

Lemmy's ears pricked up, his tail curled tight and he stood a little taller. "I'd like that, miss," he said. "It can get very lonely at the front desk sometimes."

"I plan to change that," said Anna.

And so, for the rest of the day, they worked their arms off, dusting this and scrubbing that. Up ladders, down on their knees, the team didn't stop. By evening the lobby was as bright as a glorious summer's day. There was not a speck of dust to be seen.

"I bet it's not been like this since the grand opening!" said Lemmy proudly.

T. Bear looked lost in memories, or maybe he was just very tired. He nodded in agreement.

Anna was very happy with their day's work. It was just the beginning, but at least it *was* a beginning, she thought.

Anna was all set to relax when she heard a door slam upstairs.

"Did you hear that, Lemmy?" she asked fearfully.

Lemmy's large ears twisted and turned like satellite dishes searching for signals. "There are footsteps . . ." he said.

"A burglar?" said Anna.

Anna nudged T. Bear into life. Though he was old, T. Bear was large and imposing and scared of nothing. He crept to the foot of the staircase, listening hard. Dull, scraping footsteps grew closer.

"There's definitely someone up there," he said in a low, growling sort of way.

They heard a bright ding sound up above.

"Whoever it is seems to be using the elevator," said Lemmy. "Do burglars use elevators?"

Anna crept behind T. Bear.

"Don't worry, miss," he said. "No uninvited guest has ever gotten past me."

They listened as the elevator traveled slowly down from floor to floor. The door chimed and, with a clunking clatter, it opened.

"Good evening," said a very old, very well-dressed tortoise. "It is evening, isn't it?"

Her eyes were blinking in the light as she shuffled out of the elevator using a walking stick for balance.

"Have I missed supper, dear?" she asked.

TING!
Bingo
6p.m.
Piano
Lounge

Anna felt a little more brave and left T. Bear's shadow.

"Were you upstairs?" she asked.

"Oh yes, my love," the tortoise said. "Room 202 – I think I've been asleep for quite a while. Are you new here?"

A flash of recognition crossed Lemmy's face. He was very good with guests.

"Mrs. Turpington?" he said.

"That's right, my dear," she replied. "I'm sorry, I can't remember your name . . . Hibernation does funny things to one's head."

"It's Lemmy," he said, rushing to take her arm like a gentleman. "Let me find you a seat, madam."

"But that means . . ." said Anna, doing the math, "you've been asleep for three years?"

"Heavens," said Mrs. Turpington, "is it that long? I only usually hibernate for a season, but I guess the comfort of this lovely hotel got the better of me."

"I think our hotel has changed a bit since you last saw it," said Anna sadly.

"I'm sure it has," said the tortoise, "but it also means I must owe you an awful lot of money. Will you work it out for me, and add it to my weekly bill?"

"I would be glad to," said Anna.

"Excellent, my dear," said the tortoise. "And now, I wonder, is there any chance of some lettuce soup?"

Anna's brain was whirring at such a rate that she almost couldn't contain her thoughts. With three years of money owed they might be able to hire some new staff. Maybe Mrs. Turpington was the answer to all their problems?

"I'm sure we can arrange something," said Anna, trying not to pop with joy. "Can't we, Mr. Bear?"

"Me?" he whispered. "With these giant paws?"

Anna nodded furiously.

"I-I'll do my best . . ." he stuttered.

Lemmy helped Mrs. Turpington into a

freshly cleaned chair in the lobby, and T. Bear started thinking about the best way to cook lettuce soup.

Anna raced off to the office. She closed the door and started dancing on the spot. She had her very first guest to look after. Hotel Flamingo was back in business!

Advertisements and Aardvarks

"Morning, miss," said Lemmy, as he arrived for work the next day bright and early.

Lemmy was far more alert than the previous day, unlike Anna, who was fast asleep in the corner of the dining room, propped up by the vacuum cleaner in her hands. Her eyes snapped open.

"Lemmy . . ." she said in a daze. "Time for bed?"

"It's the morning, miss," he said. "Were you cleaning all night? Mrs. Turpington will be down soon . . . I'll get the kettle on."

Anna zigzagged across the room as she came to terms with the day. T. Bear met her in the lobby. He was clutching something red.

"Good morning, miss," he said happily. His cheeks were full of color, and after the joy of the previous day he felt like a new bear. "I found this for you. So that you feel like one of the team."

T. Bear was holding a hotel uniform and a tiny red hat. Anna thought it looked wonderful.

"Thank you, Mr. Bear!" she said.

"I also made a name badge for you, and tidied your office," he said. "We can't have the manager of Hotel Flamingo working in a dustbin, can we?"

"I suppose not," said Anna.

She walked into her new office and felt overjoyed. It was so clean and tidy, and even better than that, it didn't smell of moldy socks anymore.

She hurriedly changed into her uniform. It was a little large, having been sewn for a rabbit waitress (called Bunny – according to the name tag), but Anna didn't mind. The uniform made her look and feel very important. She was ready to make decisions.

"The first thing we do today is hire new staff," she said. "Everything that's broken must be fixed."

"Yes, miss!" said T. Bear. "But how do we do that?"

"With an advertisement," said Anna, sitting proudly at her spotless desk. "I shall write one now."

T. Bear made copies of the advertisements and posted them on lampposts and billboards along Animal Boulevard. Within minutes of him returning to the hotel the reception phone was ringing – and it didn't stop until lunchtime, with each caller asking about a job.

T. Bear couldn't believe it when his broken doorway was blocked with hopeful new animals looking for work. There were aardvarks, monkeys, elephants . . . animals of all shapes and sizes.

"We really must get the revolving door working, Miss Anna," he said, lost amid a crowd of animals.

A giraffe, stooping to squeeze through the gap, raised her neck above everyone.

"I could fix it for you," she said loudly.

"Excuse me?" said Anna, peering up.

"The revolving door," said the giraffe. "I'm a handywoman. Stella's the name. I mend things."

T. Bear looked hopefully at Anna, and made a gravelly-sounding whimper. She could tell it would make him very happy to have his door working again.

"We do have a few maintenance issues," said Anna, considering the broken windows, the leaky swimming pool and the holey tennis court.

"Oh yeah. I'm good with all maintenance issues," said Stella. "My tools are in the van. I could crack on, if you'd like?"

"OK then," Anna said, liking Stella's confidence. "Treat it as your interview. If you can fix our revolving door, the job's yours."

The giraffe saluted in agreement.

"Thank you, Stella," said Anna.

"Don't you worry yourself," she replied, before ducking out of the door.

Stella was keen to get things done, and that impressed Anna more than anything.

Before long, the revolving door was fixed, and the line of animals stretched through the lobby and out into the dining room. To save time, Lemmy called them, two by two, into the office.

Anna was interviewing all afternoon, and once her mind was made up she asked the successful candidates to stay behind.

The chosen few were:

Madame Le Pig, a world-famous chef, who was terrifying, but brilliant.

Eva Koala, an unusually lively and cheerful koala, who was perfect to serve and cater for guests in the restaurant.

Squeak, a quiet and retiring old mouse, who was a fully trained bellboy and elevator operator.

Hilary Hippo,
a laundry and
cleaning specialist
with a firm dislike
of mess and dirt.

Stella Giraffe, an
expert handywoman,
good with a hammer
and drill.

SNIFF!

5
The New Team

"Welcome to Hotel Flamingo!" said Anna, addressing her new staff in the lobby with a broad smile on her face. "This is the sunniest hotel on Animal Boulevard, and it is your job to keep the sun shining."

Lemmy appeared, carrying uniforms for everyone. He handed them out, trying very hard to match each animal with

their correct shape and size of outfit.

"Good to have you all on the team," he said happily with his tail raised high. Lemmy was quickly getting back into the swing of things, and the excitement of the day had more than made up for the past three years of silence. He was feeling like a new lemur again.

As for T. Bear, he was standing proudly alongside his working revolving door. Meeting and greeting guests was what he cared most about, and he found it impossible to shake the smile from his face.

Everything was going to plan, thought Anna, but she hadn't quite bargained on

Madame Le Pig.

"SO! Where is my kitchen?" demanded the chef, stamping her trotters. "I have an amazing menu to create!"

Everyone started to quiver. Her snort was that scary.

"Over there . . ." said Anna, pointing.

"I will say this only once," added Madame Le Pig, stomping off. "DO NOT DISTURB ME WHEN I AM COOKING!"

"Excuse me? Can I go and stand in the elevator?" asked Squeak, trembling. Squeak loved peace and quiet, which is why a job in an elevator was his perfect career. And he wanted to be as far away from Madame Le Pig as any mouse could be.

Anna understood completely. "Of course," she said.

Hilary Hippo was caught mid-sneeze, and was growing redder by the second.

"Are you all right, Hilary?" asked Anna.

"In this terribly – A-A-ACHOOO! – dirty room?" sneezed Hilary.

"What do you mean, dirty?" said Anna.

"Can't you see the dust?" said Hilary. She sneezed loudly once more. "It's everywhere!"

If there was anything that got on Hilary's nerves, it was dirt. The faintest speck of mud on a carpet? Hilary could smell it. An old cobweb dangling from a light bulb? Hilary could hear it swinging in the breeze.

"Where is the vacuum cleaner?" Hilary said in between bouts of sneezing. "I can't stand it anymore! Hurry, before I die!"

Anna was dismayed at the thought she'd done a bad job of cleaning the lobby – however, this was exactly the attitude she wanted in her staff: perfection. She pointed to a storage cupboard, and Hilary got to work.

"Would anyone like a glass of sparkling water?" asked Eva Koala, who had already begun her job too. Nothing phased Eva, not even the temper of Madame Le Pig. "A juice? Or maybe some raw nuts?"

"Water, thanks," said Anna, incredibly pleased to find that Eva had taken the initiative to get started. She reached for a glass and took a gulp.

"Enjoy!" said Eva, bouncing off to the restaurant.

"What next for me, then?" asked Stella, waving a hammer.

"What are all these maintenance problems you've got? I'll have to give them a good looking over."

Anna was almost lost for words. The staff had taken to their roles with such enthusiasm!

"Oh, I have a long list," said Anna, "but first of all, the outside could do with a lick of paint. I know the perfect color – the bright blue of the sea!"

Stella rubbed her hooves together. "Right you are!" she said.

T. Bear walked over to Anna and placed his large paw on her shoulder.

"You've brought the sunshine back to our hotel," he said, smiling.

"Now I just need to bring guests . . . ." said Anna.

The elevator chimed, and its door opened. Mrs. Turpington walked out, aided by Squeak.

"Hello, my dear," said the stately tortoise. "What a good idea to have a bellboy in the elevator . . . Oh, have I missed supper again?"

"No, no, not at all," said Anna.

She glanced at the kitchens and elbowed T. Bear.

"Would you ask Madame Le Pig if she's ready to cook our guest some lettuce soup?" she said.

T. Bear made a loud, ominous gulp.

"I'm just the doorbear," he said sheepishly, and walked back toward his revolving doors.

Anna realized she'd have to face Madame Le Pig sooner or later. She steeled herself and hurried off to see how her new chef was faring.

"Excuse me," said Anna meekly, opening the kitchen door. "Might you be able to cook some lettuce soup for our guest?"

Madame Le Pig was scribbling furiously, inventing a new recipe to wow her guests. She snorted angrily. "I am trying to work!" she spat.

"I thought cooking was your work, madame," said Anna, trying to remember that it was she who ran the hotel.

"You will call me Madame Le Pig!" Le

Pig replied. "Yes, cooking IS my work. But first I must know what to cook. And that is what I am doing – writing my menu, which will bring you awards and respect for this tiny, smelly old establishment! Do not disturb me again!"

Anna was a little alarmed by Madame Le Pig, but decided not to push it any further. The key to good management, she was quickly learning, was to give

people space to do their job.

Anna returned to T. Bear and asked him very kindly if he would make some more lettuce soup as Madame Le Pig was busy. Thankfully for everyone, he was happy to oblige.

With the staff now busily going about their jobs Anna realized it was time to find herself a bedroom. The day had gotten the better of her, and she was exhausted.

Lemmy showed her to the staff quarters in the basement of the hotel. It was dark and dank in the basement, but there were many empty rooms. Anna picked one with a little window near the ceiling, which looked out over the pavement at foot height.

Though her room was dimly lit and the iron bed creaked with the slightest touch, Anna was delighted. In time she would decorate it, and it would look just like home.

She folded her clothes away neatly and placed the old photo of her hotel on

the bedside table. One day, she promised herself, Hotel Flamingo would be back to its glorious old ways.

And with the lights off and the rumble of traffic humming in the background, Anna fell asleep.

WHIRRRR!

6

The Pink Flamingos

Morning arrived with the sound of sneezing and the hum of a vacuum cleaner.

Anna pried apart her eyes, dressed quickly and opened her door. She found Hilary Hippo hard at work, looking rather flustered.

"I don't know how anyone sleeps when there's so much cleaning to be done!" said Hilary, bumping the vacuum cleaner along the poky corridor. "Even the dust is dusty!"

"I admit, it is a never-ending job," said Anna.

"It certainly is not!" said Hilary. "And I'll know it's done when I stop sneezing. My nose is very delicate."

Anna was impressed that a hippo's nose, so vast and so noticeable, could be so delicate.

"Ah, well, thank you," said Anna.

Hilary meandered on, still sneezing, still cleaning.

Hotel Flamingo was full of staff, but in order to keep it that way Anna now needed to fill it with guests. Forever present at the back of her mind was the threat of their competition on the hill. The Glitz, with its extravagant decor and thrilling entertainment, offered so much that Hotel Flamingo couldn't. This problem of guests would be a lot harder to solve, she thought.

Everyone was hard at work upstairs too. Eva Koala had prepared the dining room for breakfast, and the kitchen was steaming and noisy, full of the clatter of pots and pans. Though they had just one guest – who only ate leaves – Anna was thrilled to smell breakfast cooking.

"Hey, Anna!" said Stella, who was dressed in paint-splattered gray overalls.

CLAP!
CLAP!

“Come and look. It’s much better now, if I do say so myself.”

Anna raced through the revolving doors, passing T. Bear on the way, and jumped out onto the pavement. The sky was clear and the air was as crisp as a lettuce. The hotel was now a rich shade of blue, as magnificent as the sea, and exactly as Anna had imagined.

“I LOVE IT!” she cried.

Stella blushed at the compliment. “That’s what you pay me for,” she said. “And I also found this in the storage cupboard downstairs.”

Stella passed Anna a life-size pink plastic flamingo, which had seen better days. Its beak was cracked, its wing was hanging on by a wire and one leg looked likely to fall off.

"I think it should be up there with the sign," said Stella. "Want me to fix it?"

Anna froze. The statue had suddenly given her an outrageous idea. She leapt with joy, and kissed the flamingo's broken beak.

"You bet I would," she cried, and hurried back indoors.

Anna headed into her office and slammed the door shut. She needed total quiet to think. Her brain whirred, her pencil hand scribbled, and within minutes she knew exactly what it was she needed to do. She needed to think big and act big.

"Lemmy!" she shouted.

The lemur quickly appeared at the door. "Morning, miss," he said. "Can I help?"

"How many pink flamingos do you know?" she asked.

Lemmy scratched his head. It wasn't an everyday question.

"Not many . . ." he said. "Although my sister once starred alongside one in a play. I could try her?"

"Give her a call!" said Anna. "I need as many flamingos as we can muster. I have a BIG idea."

"Yes, miss," he said, returning to the lobby.

Anna tapped her pencil on her desk as Lemmy dialed numbers on the phone. She waited impatiently. He started talking. Another call later, he returned.

"You're in luck," said Lemmy. "I've just been chatting to a Ms. Fragranti, the founder of a stage school for pink flamingos. If you want pink flamingos, you've got pink flamingos."

Anna punched the air. "YES!" she

cried. "Invite her and her whole school to stay – a free vacation, if you like. In return, all I ask is that they help promote our hotel. The hotel will look busy, and we'll get some free advertising."

"I'll get on to it," said Lemmy, smiling. He stopped to ask another question. "You have dealt with flamingos before, though, right?"

"What do you mean?" said Anna.

Lemmy thought over his answer. "They're . . . Well, they can be a little difficult," he said.

"How difficult can they be?" said Anna.

Lemmy smiled. "I guess you're about to find out," he said.

New Arrivals

DING!

The bell rang at the front desk, but Lemmy couldn't see anyone there at all.

"Hello?" he said, turning his head from left to right.

T. Bear shrugged by the door. He'd let no one in.

"Excuse us?" said a choir of tiny voices.

Lemmy peered over the desk and saw

a group of cockroaches with bags and suitcases, waiting to be served.

"Good morning, my friend," said a tall, well-to-do cockroach, removing his top hat with a flourish. "I don't suppose you'd have a room to spare? They don't allow our kind at the Glitz, and there's nowhere else for us to go. We deserve a vacation too, you know."

Anna overheard the conversation and left her office. Why would the Glitz turn

away paying guests? she wondered. It made no sense!

"Of course we have a room," said Anna, kneeling down to get a closer look. "Everyone is welcome here at Hotel Flamingo."

"Err," said Lemmy. He pulled Anna to one side and whispered in her ear, "We've not had insects before – do they get a normal room? How will they open the door?"

Anna didn't know the first thing about insects nor, come to think of it, most animals. She had a lot to learn.

"Will you all be staying in the one room?" she asked the tall cockroach.

"That suits us perfectly, yes," he replied, and offered up his tiny passport and

210

miniature credit card. Anna took them carefully so as not to lose them, and signed the creatures in.

"Thank you, Mr. Roachford," said Anna, squinting to read his details. She handed over a door key, which needed four of the insects to carry it. "Room 210. You may find the bed a little large for your liking, but do let us know if we can make things better. I hope you enjoy your stay."

"I'll carry your bags, sir," said Lemmy, picking them up in the palm of one hand. He liked guests who traveled light.

The crowd of cockroaches scuttled off toward the elevator and Lemmy saw them inside.

"Second floor, please," he said to Squeak.

"Certainly, yes," said the mouse,

nodding to the cockroaches.

As the elevator closed, Lemmy returned to the desk.

"I just hope insects like sheets on their beds," said Anna.

"You'll soon find that paying guests will tell you if things aren't to their liking," said Lemmy. "You can be sure of that!"

•

Late that afternoon, T. Bear was shocked to find a flock of pink flamingos massing outside the hotel. They'd flown in from afar and were blocking Animal Boulevard. Trucks, vans and cars couldn't pass, and their drivers were

honking and hooting their angry thoughts.

"Miss Anna . . ." said T. Bear. "You might want to come and see this!"

Anna ran from her office to see the colorful spectacle. She quickly gathered her clipboard and walked out to greet her new guests.

"Ahh! Ms. Fragranti!" she said.

The flamingos were dressed in swimming gear and sunglasses, and were loaded with luggage – they were clearly ready for a vacation.

A very tall, slender flamingo with a feathered hat turned to face Anna. "What a marvelous establishment, darling!" said Ms. Fragranti, dancing closer on her long legs. "Your offer is most welcome. We birds do love a working vacation."

"It is our pleasure," said Anna. "If you head on in, we'll give you your rooms. We have plenty of spare beds."

Ms. Fragranti looked concerned. "Beds, darling?" she said.

"Yes, of course," said Anna. "We have enough to go around."

"You do know we sleep on our feet? And we certainly don't need rooms," replied Ms. Fragranti. "We need a lake, or at least a pool."

It was the cockroach problem all over again, thought Anna. Every animal had different needs and she hadn't a clue what they were. She realized she had to do some research, and quick!

"Of-of course I knew that," she stuttered. "We have a pool; it'll soon be ready for you . . ." Anna turned to head back inside. "Anyway, please come on in and get refreshed," she said. "You must be exhausted after your flight?"

"Three hours nonstop, darling," said Ms. Fragranti, wafting her wings dramatically, "and my wings are close to dropping off!"

T. Bear ushered the flamingos inside and called on Eva Koala to get drinks. Anna hurried off to find Stella and hoped that the swimming pool could be repaired. What on earth would she do if not?

BUG

8

A Pig and a Poke

Anna was sitting in her office reading about cockroaches when Madame Le Pig barged in.

"You expect me – ME! – to feed flamingos?" she squealed. "Do you know what they eat?"

"Er . . ." began Anna.

"They eat tiny slimy water thingies," said Madame Le Pig. "I do not cook these tiny

water thingies, you hear?! I cannot even see these thingies to cook – they are so tiny!"

"What *do* you cook then, chef?" asked Anna.

"I prepare food. PROPER FOOD! Cakes! Soufflé! Crème brûlée!" argued Le Pig.

Anna had no idea what they were, let alone how to spell them.

"Can't you make crème brûlée with tiny water-based thingies?" she asked hopefully.

Madame Le Pig's

eyes lit up with fire. Anna had clearly said the wrong thing.

"Crème brûlée is a pudding with crunchy sugar topping!" screamed Le Pig. "Would you eat a fish pudding?"

Anna shrunk back into her chair. Chef was right, it sounded disgusting.

"Just make sure there is some food they can eat, please, Madame Le Pig," she asked very nicely. "Everyone will be wanting breakfast tomorrow."

Madame Le Pig stomped off, fuming. "You shall get your wish!" she snorted.

Anna was beginning to wonder whether she'd made the right decision in hiring such a grumpy chef. But with a party of cockroaches, a group of flamingos and a tortoise to cater for, there was no way she could get rid of her. Besides, having to tell her to leave would be far worse than not having a chef at all!

•

Anna walked onto the garden terrace to

see how Stella was getting on with the pool. A huddle of young flamingos were watching poolside, sipping from brightly colored drinks. They seemed happy, despite not having any water to stand in.

Stella's long neck towered out of the pool while her unseen arms were hammering away on the tiled floor.

"How's it looking?" asked Anna. The responsibility of caring for her guests was starting to weigh on her – not that she'd let it show.

"Well, I think the leaks are fixed," said Stella, sucking in breath, "but now the water pipe is blocked, so we can't fill it."

"How do you unblock a pipe?" asked Anna.

"That's a very good question," said Stella. "I mean, it all depends on what's blocking it. I could try poking a stick in it, but that could make things worse!"

Anna sighed. She needed Ms. Fragranti and the flamingos to help her bring guests to the hotel – she had to get the pool repaired.

"Leave it with me," she said. But Anna hadn't the first idea what to do.

She entered the lobby and collapsed into a chair. Running a hotel had seemed like such a good idea a few days ago, but now not so much. How could she unblock the pipe? Had she taken on far too much?

T. Bear could tell something was wrong. "What's on your mind, miss?" he said, walking over.

"I don't know what I'm doing," said Anna. "I always know what to do, but today . . . I'm starting to feel out of my depth."

"Miss Anna," said T. Bear kindly, "without you Hotel Flamingo would still be rotting away. Look at it now! It's busy once more!"

The group of cockroaches scampered into view, chatting away, having a great time.

"Look how happy Mr. Roachford and his party is," said T. Bear. "All because of you."

"But the water pipe is blocked," said Anna. "The flamingos will all go home without the pool."

Mr. Roachford's head pricked up. He turned to Anna. "Sorry to interrupt," he said with immaculate manners, "but did I hear word of a blocked pipe?"

"Yes," she replied, "so we can't fill the pool."

"One moment," said Mr. Roachford, and he left to discuss matters with his friends.

"Would you mind terribly if we took a look?" he asked upon his return. "There's nothing a cockroach likes more than an adventure through sewers."

"Do you mean it?" Anna asked.

"Very much so," said Mr. Roachford.

Anna was amazed by how generous cockroaches were.

"Thank you, Mr. Roachford!" she said.

T. Bear smiled and returned to his post as Anna led the cockroaches out to the pool.

The insects disappeared down the water pipe under the watchful eye of Stella.

"Don't get lost!" she said.

"Oh, we won't!" said Mr. Roachford.

Stella and Anna waited anxiously. They could hear the tikker-takker of tiny insect feet echoing through the pipe. Minutes passed without a word. And then they returned.

"Now then," said Mr. Roachford, removing his top hat. "You have a slight problem. It would appear that you have a bad case of squatters in your water system."

9

Uninvited Guests

"Excuse me," said Anna, peering down the drain. "But this is a hotel. Whoever's down there, I'm afraid that you can't stay."

A glistening sea otter's head popped out of the pipe. Her cheeky face and cute little nose didn't reflect her punchy attitude.

"HA! Not squatters," said Stella. "Otters!"

"What do you mean we can't stay?" squeaked the indignant otter. "We've been here for over a year. It's our home. We know our rights!"

"I need to fill the swimming pool for our guests," said Anna, trying to sound reasonable.

"Pool?" said the otter.

"Yes, and you're blocking the water pipes," said Anna. "I can't fill the pool with you in there."

"Well, what do you expect *me* to do about it?" said the otter.

Anna breathed deeply. "Move?" she suggested.

"Where to?" said the sea otter. "I have

a family – three children to look after. I can't afford the rents on Animal Boulevard."

Anna could see a compromise was in order.

"I have an idea," she said. "If you let me get the pool working, you can stay in the hotel. We have many rooms, but you will have to work for your rent."

"What sort of work?" asked the otter.

"It could be the perfect job," said Anna. "Do you like to swim?"

The otter laughed. "You're asking an otter if they like to swim?"

"Yes," said Anna. "With the pool full again we'll need a lifeguard who's a good swimmer. Someone such as an otter?"

The otter liked the sound of that.

"Oh. You're right. That is perfect," she said.

"I thought it might be," said Anna.

The otter disappeared underground, and within seconds chairs, tables and beds were being thrown out of the drain. These were followed by three young otters, all carrying suitcases and cuddly toys.

"My name's Jojo," said the otter. "You've got a deal."

Anna shook Jojo's paw. "Good to have you on the team," she said. "I'll get you whatever you need!"

It was only once she'd said it that Anna realized she had no idea what a sea otter *would* need.

"We'll need oysters, of course," said Jojo. "And some seaweed in the bath. It's excellent for our coats."

"Seaweed?" said Anna.

"Freshly cut," said Jojo.

As Anna wondered how on earth she was going to get a supply of freshly cut seaweed, the pipe rumbled and a stream of water flew out into the pool.

The flamingos cheered in celebration and leapt in, feet first.

Anna found Mr. Roachford, to thank him.

"I'm so grateful to you," she said.

"Oh please, it's the least we could do," he replied. "You've been so kind to us. This is our favorite hotel in the world."

His words made Anna glow with pride.

•

That evening, as the sun started to set, Anna found Ms. Fragranti relaxing in the pool. She was resting on one leg, reading *The Color of Shrimp*, a guide to flamingo feather coloring.

"Could I have a word?" asked Anna.

Ms. Fragranti's head reared up from the pages. "But of course, darling," she said, clutching her heart.

"The reason I wanted you here is that you are the perfect advertisement for our hotel," said Anna. "We need to tell the world that we're fully open for business, and you're the creatures to do it."

"I should say so, darling!" said Ms. Fragranti, performing a pirouette. "But what would you like us to do?"

"I thought you could hand out some leaflets," said Anna.

"Well, we can certainly do that," said Ms. Fragranti, "but I have a far better idea too. Why don't we perform our show? That's what you really want us to do, isn't it, darling?"

"Your show? Here?" asked Anna.

"But of course, darling!" said Ms. Fragranti. "In the Piano Lounge. A gala performance would bring in some new guests, yes? And they could see how lovely your hotel is, while enjoying some wonderful acting."

Anna couldn't believe her luck. She didn't need to think it over.

"Could the show be ready by tomorrow evening?" asked Anna.

"We're always ready, darling."

"I'll prepare the leaflets," said Anna happily. "This is just perfect!"

•

As the hotel guests made their way to bed, T. Bear helped a hunched gray cat through the revolving door. Dressed in a raincoat and carrying a briefcase, the cat's gaze darted left to right as though looking for clues at a crime scene.

"Traveled far?" asked T. Bear.

"No," said the cat in a rich, hushed voice. He smoothed back his ears. "I need a room. I take it you have one free?"

"I'm sure we do, sir," he replied. "Head to the desk where Mr. Lemmy will be pleased to help you."

The cat nodded in thanks and walked into the lobby.

"Room for one. Two nights only," said the cat.

"Yes, sir," said Lemmy. "And your name?"

"Mr. Grayson," said the cat. "I want a quiet room. No disturbances. A saucer of milk left outside my door at sunrise, and breakfast at seven a.m. Litter tray, not toilet – cleaned twice daily."

"Certainly, sir," said Lemmy, hastily filling out the entry in the guest book. He handed over a key, and pointed to the breakfast room. "Breakfast is served through there."

The elevator chimed and Anna walked out as Mr. Grayson slipped by and up the staircase.

"Who was that?" asked Anna, surprised by the arrival of another new guest, and at such a late hour.

"One Mr. Grayson," Lemmy said, shrugging. "Odd sort. Seemed to be watching my every movement. But then this is a hotel. You get some funny types at a place like this."

"I'm starting to understand that," said Anna.

She watched Mr. Grayson travel up the stairs gracefully. He rubbed his paw along the underside of the banister as though searching for dust. *What is he up to?* thought Anna. She decided to keep a very close eye on him.

PIANO LOUNGE
TONIGHT!
AMAZING
GALA FLAMINGO
PERFORMANCE
- Ms Dupont ♡

10

A Cat Among the Pigeons

The next morning, Anna put up a poster in the lobby of the hotel.

Madame Le Pig had stayed true to her word. There was food for everyone, and for the first time in years the restaurant was buzzing during breakfast – and it wasn't because of flies. Eva worked tirelessly serving food, never seeming to care about Madame Le Pig's attitude.

Anna watched from afar. Mrs. Turpington was happily enjoying a lettuce tea, the cockroaches were nibbling pastries, and the flamingos were slurping some sort of fish porridge. Though it looked horrible to Anna, she was pleased to see that Madame Le Pig had made something especially for them.

And then Mr. Grayson, the cat, arrived for his breakfast, wearing exactly the same outfit as the previous day, and still carrying his briefcase.

"Good morning, sir," said Anna, showing him to a seat. "What can I get you for breakfast?"

Mr. Grayson sat down. He looked at the menu snootily.

"Do you have kippers?" he purred languidly. "I want kippers. I like them

rare, in a tomato sauce. Not too much salt. A tiny sprinkling of pepper."

"Yes, sir," said Anna. "I'll see what's available."

Anna entered the kitchen. Madame Le Pig was in a horrendous mood.

"NO!" she shouted. "WE DO NOT HAVE THE KIPPERS. WE HAVE

WHAT IS ON THE MENU!"

"But Mr. Grayson has asked for them," said Anna.

Madame Le Pig went suddenly pale. "Mr. Grayson?" she whispered. "A pussycat? In a raincoat?"

"That's right," said Anna.

Madame Le Pig paced around her kitchen, rubbing her trotters together anxiously. "You know who this is?" said Le Pig. "He is the famous hotel inspector. He has the power to shut down hotels!"

"He ha the ower to do what?" said Anna.

"SHUT US DOWN!" said Madame Le Pig. "He can close Hotel Flamingo if he finds anything he doesn't like!"

"Oh, goodness," said Anna. "Are you

sure you don't have kippers?"

Madame Le Pig snorted and clapped her trotters together. She took a deep breath. "Yes, I have the kippers," she said. "Now. OUT OF MY KITCHEN!"

•

After breakfast, Anna called a meeting.

"We have a hotel inspector staying with us," she said ominously.

Her staff looked shocked.

"Mr. Grayson?" said Lemmy.

"That's him," said Anna.

"I knew there was something odd about that cat," said T. Bear.

"So even though we're all working especially hard right now," said Anna, "we all have to work even harder. Our jobs depend on it."

Ms. Fragranti had decided to come to the meeting, even though she wasn't an official staff member.

"When he sees our show, darling, you won't need to worry anymore!" she said, curling her neck theatrically.

Anna nodded. "I hope so – but safety, cleanliness and tidiness are equally important," said Anna. "We have to be on our best form."

The hotel staff agreed to double their efforts.

"And, Mr. Lemmy," said Anna, "I'd like you to pay very close attention to everything Mr. Grayson does. Don't let him out of your sight!"

"Yes, miss!" said Lemmy.

They all went their separate ways, determined to impress the inspector.

"I mustn't let a single guest down," said Anna, and she set to checking on everyone herself, from the cockroaches to the flamingos. She knew there would be no rest until Mr. Grayson had left.

DIN-DINS
GARLIC

11
On the Streets

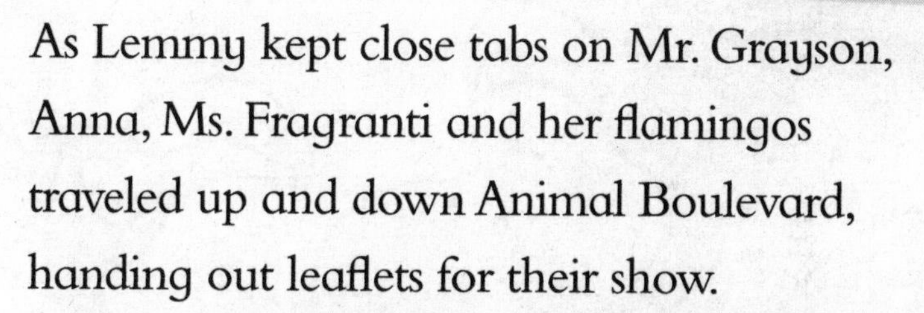

As Lemmy kept close tabs on Mr. Grayson, Anna, Ms. Fragranti and her flamingos traveled up and down Animal Boulevard, handing out leaflets for their show.

The palm-lined road was bustling with tourists. Packed with splendid shops, bars and cafes – from Slippy Seal's Seaweed Store to the world-famous Oyster Bazaar & Cafe – Anna found she could buy almost everything she needed to meet her guests' and staff's needs. *Jojo and her otters will be pleased*, thought Anna.

And just when Anna thought the day couldn't get any better, the flamingos proved excellent at selling themselves.

"Come to our show! Hotel Flamingo!" they sang as they flooded the area. They were unmissable. Their brilliant-pink feathers made them stand out from all the other animals on the road. Anna needed to do nothing but watch as they handed out leaflets and convinced animals to visit.

Animal Boulevard was a long stretch of headland that jutted out into the sea, bordered by sandy beaches on each side.

The road traveled all the way up onto the hill, where, at its end, was the Glitz hotel. The hotel taunted Anna from afar with its riches.

"I can't believe we're up against that hotel," said Anna, sighing.

"They may have money," said Ms. Fragranti, "but they don't have your style, darling – nor flamingos! Besides, your hotel is so warm and welcoming."

"Thank you," said Anna, though she knew she'd need both style *and* money for the hotel to thrive.

"One thing I've always found in this business," said Ms. Fragranti, gesturing flamboyantly with a wing, "is that you need friends to succeed. Look after your friends, darling, and your friends will look after you."

Anna took that advice to heart. "If we make this work," she said, "you shall be forever welcome at my hotel."

"It will work, Anna, darling," said the flamingo. "There's no question of that. Now, off you go. I've got one last animal I need to see," she added with a wink.

"Who?" asked Anna, wondering why Ms. Fragranti had suddenly become all secretive.

"Do not worry. All will be well, darling," she said. "You'll see. Curtains up at eight p.m. sharp in the Piano Lounge!"

•

Lemmy watched Mr. Grayson all day long. The cat carried a notebook wherever he went, jotting down notes at every corner, stairwell and window.

Mr. Grayson even took a dip in the pool – cared for by Jojo and her young otters – which was now so impressively clean you could take a bath in it.

As dinnertime approached, Lemmy relayed all the events to Anna, who was desperate to know how the day had gone.

"Mr. Grayson lay on that float in the pool for close to an hour!" Lemmy told her.

"Do cats like to swim?" asked Anna.

“Some of them,” said Lemmy. “Although he didn’t like being splashed by the flamingos.”

“They splashed him?” cringed Anna.

“I’m sure it was only a little drip,” said Lemmy.

“You’re absolutely sure?” said Anna.

“Totally,” said Lemmy. “He did mention tonight’s show, though. He’s expecting great things from our Ms. Fragranti.”

“He is?” said Anna, her worry building. “Oh, I hope they’re good.”

“They should be, they’ve been rehearsing for hours!” said Lemmy. “Which is just as well, as we’ve got a dozen reservations for dinner already.”

SILENCE!
REHEARSALS
IN PROGRESS
SCRIPT

Anna thought she'd heard wrong. "For dinner, here?"

"That's right. Animals are coming to see the show," said Lemmy, grinning from ear to ear. "Your flamingo plan has worked a treat."

Anna skipped through the lobby. In the Piano Lounge T. Bear was helping Stella erect a stage, and Hilary Hippo was cleaning the seats, placing flowers on each one. Three flamingos were busy practicing their lines.

"Break a leg!" said Anna, though she immediately wondered if that was the correct thing to say to a flamingo actor. *They do have such beautiful long legs*, thought Anna, *it would be awful to hurt one*.

The birds smiled, reassuring Anna, but

that feeling was short-lived. Mr. Grayson had been watching the rehearsal, and was now lurking at the back of the lounge, staring through a magnifying glass at one of the ornate light fixtures.

"Everything to your liking, sir?" asked Anna.

Mr. Grayson nodded, unhappy at being spotted, and slunk off. Anna knew the future of the hotel rested on the coming night, and as every minute passed there was less and less she could do about it.

12

Taking on the Glitz

Anna was helping Eva set tables in the restaurant when she heard a rowdy kerfuffle in the lobby.

"Oh goodness, what's that? Not tonight!" she said, running out.

Lemmy and T. Bear were trying to stop a posse of heavy-set dogs from entering the hotel, but they were having little effect. In the middle of them was a brute of a lion dressed up in a fine suit and cravat.

"Can I help you?" asked Anna.

"Am I speaking to the owner?" asked the lion.

"You are," said Anna.

"I am Ronald Ruffian," said the lion, flicking back his mane. "I own the Glitz. I'm sure you've heard of me."

Anna was struck by a lightning bolt of fear. This was the animal that had almost destroyed Hotel Flamingo! What was he doing here?

"And I am Anna Dupont," she said, sounding as confident as she could manage. "Welcome to Hotel Flamingo, the sunniest hotel on Animal Boulevard."

"I'll be the judge of that," said Ruffian. "I have a table booked for dinner."

"You have?" said Anna.

But Mr. Ruffian was already striding through into the restaurant as if he owned the place.

"You could have warned me!" hissed Anna to Lemmy.

"I didn't know!" said the lemur. "Honest!"

The evening was getting worse by the second.

And then Mr. Grayson appeared from the staircase.

"Good evening, sir," said Anna, feeling distinctly on edge. "Dinner?"

The cat nodded and proceeded through to the restaurant.

More guests arrived as Anna headed into the restaurant herself. There was a giant panda in sequins led by a dashing walrus, a pair of alligators dressed in golden tuxedos, not to mention a very old goose with a diamond necklace. The great and good of Animal Boulevard

were in Anna's hotel, and she could barely contain her excitement.

It was truly busy and the atmosphere was electric. Eva was rushed off her feet, but loving every minute of it. She ferried plates of astounding-looking food back and forth, a smile always on her face. Each time she opened the swinging doors to the kitchen, puffs of steam and smoke gushed out. Anna could see there was a buildup of dishes ready to bring out to guests.

"Can I help?" asked Anna.

"You bet," said Eva. "It sure is busy."

Anna took a notebook and pencil, donned a white apron and set to work reading the menu to get acquainted with the dishes. The food Madame Le Pig had prepared was just as impressive as the chef had claimed it would be. It was a feast of epic proportions, with meals designed for all tastes and diets.

"She really is a genius," said Anna.

A bell rang – more dishes were ready for customers.

"Where are my staff?" cried Madame Le Pig.

"Coming!" said Anna.

But Anna had barely moved an inch before Mr. Ruffian tapped her on the shoulder.

"I don't like sitting next to cockroaches," he complained. "They don't belong in a restaurant."

"They belong in *my* restaurant," said Anna. "Now either leave, or sit down and enjoy our hospitality."

Mr. Ruffian was not used to being spoken to in such a manner. He growled and crossed his arms. Anna winked at the table of cockroaches, who were enjoying a fine soup. Mr. Roachford tipped his hat to her in thanks. Anna was not going to let Mr. Ruffian belittle her anymore. She moved to the next table, where Mr. Grayson had been watching her. He gave her a slight smile.

"The food is excellent," he said, tucking into a medley of fish heads and rice.

"Thank you," said Anna, wanting to scream with happiness. She held it in, and escaped to the kitchen.

"HE LIKES IT!" cried Anna.

"Get out! Get out!" squealed Madame Le Pig, sorting colored vegetables onto a plate in the shape of a rainbow. "I am creating beautiful food!"

"Yes you are," said Anna happily.

Anna couldn't help but smile, and she was certain a rare glimmer of a smile also crossed Madame Le Pig's snout.

Showtime

Ms. Fragranti arrived at the restaurant door dressed in a beautiful diamond-studded outfit. She waved at Anna, who joined her.

"We are ready, darling!" said Ms. Fragranti, shaking her head so her hat feathers fluttered in the air.

"And don't you look marvelous," said Anna.

"Flamingos always look marvelous," she replied. "And I see you have a special guest here?"

"Mr. Ruffian?" said Anna. "Did you invite him?"

Ms. Fragranti laughed. "Of course I did," she said, placing her wing around Anna. "I paid him a little visit earlier on. That pompous beast needed to see how wonderful Hotel Flamingo is. It puts the Glitz to shame. Besides, I knew he wouldn't be able to resist the offer."

"Well, I should have liked to know in advance," said Anna.

"So you could worry about his visit?" said Ms. Fragranti. "No, no. All your staff and guests saw the way you dealt with him in there. You've proved yourself beyond doubt and earned their respect tonight."

"I don't know about that," said Anna.

"I do, darling," said Ms. Fragranti, twirling on one leg. "And now it's our turn to prove ourselves. Once your guests have finished eating, send them through."

One by one, the guests finished their dinners and headed to the Piano Lounge.

The room had been transformed. A glitter ball sparkled from the ceiling, and beams of light lit up the stage curtain.

All the guests were wowed by the sight – which was a surprise even for Anna. A drum rolled and T. Bear took to the stage, wearing a pink feather boa.

"I should now like to ask Hotel Flamingo's owner to come on stage and

say a few words," he said.

"Me?" said Anna, nerves suddenly turning her stomach. "Up there?"

"Miss Anna Dupont!" announced T. Bear.

The guests cheered and clapped, and Anna wanted to hide away. But as nervous as she was she couldn't say no. It was such a big moment. She took a deep breath, feeling everyone's eyes on her, and then she spoke.

"Thank you so much for coming to Hotel Flamingo," she said. "I know you will love tonight's show. It gives me great pleasure to present the best flamingos in the business . . . The Pink Feather Cabaret!"

As she left the stage a fanfare piped up. The curtains opened, and Ms. Fragranti

and her school of flamingos danced into the spotlight. They swirled in unison, their feathers blurring into a wall of color and, with Ms. Fragranti leading the proceedings, they put on a show to end all shows. There was singing, dancing and theater, just as the poster had promised.

And there was even a little magic to spice up the night.

As the curtain fell afterward the audience leapt to their feet. There were cheers and clapping from all the guests and staff.

"AMAZING!" cried Anna.

"Hoorah!" Mrs. Turpington said, laughing.

"MORE!" cried Jojo and her young sea otters.

"Encore!" chanted the cockroaches.

Mr. Ruffian pulled himself up from his chair and his bodyguard dogs surrounded him. He was furious at the show's success.

"You've made yourself a very big enemy!" he growled as he stormed out of the hotel.

Then Lemmy appeared, carrying two bouquets of flowers, and as Ms. Fragranti took a bow he clambered onto the stage to hand one to her. The other was for Anna.

"You've made us all very happy," he said as he passed her the flowers. "It's just like the old days."

Anna was overjoyed to hear this. "Thank you," she said happily. "But I could never have done it without you and everyone else."

14
The Morning After

Anna wandered sleepily into the lobby at the crack of dawn, and found Lemmy in exactly the same position as she had when she'd first arrived at Hotel Flamingo. He was leaned over the front desk, half asleep.

But this time Anna didn't poke him to wake him up. She patted him on the shoulder gently.

"You deserve a rest," she said. "I'll take over for you."

Lemmy's eyes tried to open, but they clearly didn't want to.

"Really?" he asked.

"Go and get some sleep," said Anna. So he did.

Standing behind the front desk, Anna felt over the moon. The hotel was no longer dusty and deathly quiet; it was fizzing with excitement. And it was all because of her and her new friends. What a success last night had been!

T. Bear appeared, carrying a newspaper. "Have you seen this?!" he asked.

He showed Anna a glowing review of last night's show and their hotel.

THE BEST HOTEL ON ANIMAL BOULEVARD! was the headline.

"I don't believe it," said Anna.

"Mr. Ruffian will be fuming," said T. Bear, rubbing his paws with glee.

Anna couldn't have asked for a better start to the day. But then Mr. Grayson arrived at the desk, looking stern.

"Miss Dupont, can I have a quiet word please?" he asked.

"In my office?" said Anna.

"Thank you," said Mr. Grayson.

The review was one thing, but without Mr. Grayson's approval the hotel might have to close. Anna walked nervously into her office, expecting the worst.

"Ms. Dupont," said the cat, "it's an absolute pleasure to see your hotel back to its old self again."

Anna breathed a sigh of relief.

"However," he continued, "we must discuss the matter of the insects."

"The cockroaches?" said Anna.

"As a hotel inspector," said Mr. Grayson, "I spend a lot of time looking for vermin, and infestations."

"But Mr. Roachford isn't any trouble," said Anna worriedly. Her heart started to race.

"Cockroaches are seen as dirty," said Mr. Grayson. "They can be the first sign of an unclean hotel."

"So you're closing us down?" said Anna tearfully. "Because I let Mr. Roachford and his party stay here? That's just wrong. They have just as much right as anyone to be here."

Mr. Grayson twisted his whiskers and breathed deeply. "Yes, it is wrong," he said. "Which is exactly why I plan to make an example of your hotel. I am determined to change the rules. Insects should be welcome everywhere."

"Really?" said Anna.

"Absolutely. I've seen how very pleasant Mr. Roachford and his family are. So I'm delighted to say that Hotel Flamingo passes all the checks."

"It does?" said Anna.

"Yes, it does," he replied, handing Anna a signed

certificate. "Congratulations."

Anna bounced around the office excitedly. All her hard work had been worth it. "Thank you!" she cried.

"Oh no, thank *you*," said Mr. Grayson humbly.

Anna led him from the building and, in the process, spotted Stella walking outside, carrying a ladder.

"What are you up to?" asked Anna.

Stella clambered up to the hotel sign, and put the finishing touches to the plastic pink flamingo.

"I've been fixing the sign, like you asked," she said proudly. "And now it just needs switching on."

"Really?!" said Anna.

The plastic pink flamingo was the most

perfect icing on the most perfect cake.

"Can you get everyone out here, T. Bear?" Anna called. "This is not a moment to miss!"

T. Bear rallied the staff, and when everyone was assembled outside he turned on the power.

The flamingo lit up in a burst of pink light, and Anna stepped back to get a good view. Hotel Flamingo now looked exactly as it did in the photo she'd arrived with!

"Just perfect," said Eva Koala happily.

"Marvelous, darling!" cheered Ms. Fragranti.

"Scrubs up a treat!" said Jojo.

"It will need regular cleaning," said Hilary, though she didn't sneeze.

"It is better," snorted Madame Le Pig. "Now I must get back to work."

Anna loved being around all her new friends – particularly T. Bear and Lemmy, who had made her so welcome.

"Now we're really open for business," she said proudly.

"We really are," said T. Bear. "Miss Anna, you've saved our hotel."

"We all have," said Anna.

And with a warm glow in her heart she headed back inside to the front desk, just as the phone began to ring. She crossed her fingers for luck and answered it, not knowing what to expect.

"Hello? Yes?" said Anna, grinning from ear to ear. "You'd like to make a reservation?"

And the phone rang all morning long.

HOW DID YOU FARE ON THE SNAIL TRAIL?
DID YOU FIND ALL TWENTY OF ME?

T. Bear's Lettuce Soup

(perfect for surprise tortoise guests)

YOU WILL NEED:

1 tablespoon vegetable oil
1 onion, finely chopped
1 pint vegetable stock
1 round lettuce, washed and finely shredded
3 large potatoes, peeled and chopped into very small pieces
1 sprig of chopped parsley for garnish
1 grown-up, to help

METHOD:

In a large saucepan, gently heat the vegetable oil and fry the onions until they soften. This will take 5–10 minutes. Keep the heat very low so the onions don't burn.

Now add the lettuce and potatoes and a little of the stock so that nothing sticks to the base of the pan. Stir well, then place the lid on the pan and simmer for 10 minutes.

Add the rest of the stock and simmer for a further 15 minutes.

Once cool, puree the soup in a blender until smooth.

T. Bear's Lettuce Soup can be served hot or chilled straight from the fridge. Garnish each bowl with some chopped parsley or, if you're feeling particularly adventurous (and serving the soup chilled), you could dice some cucumber into tiny cubes and add them for a refreshing burst in each mouthful!

A NOTE FROM THE AUTHOR

Writing a story about an animal hotel is a dream come true for me. I love learning about animals (my favorites are lemurs!) and I love drawing them, but I particularly love customer service.

So, as much as I'd like to stay at Hotel Flamingo and eat Madame Le Pig's amazing food, I would actually really like to work there. Yes, you heard right. Tidying the place up, planning and cooking meals, booking shows, making people happy . . . oh, that would be better than anything!

Hotel Flamingo